WORRY IS NOT WORTH WORRYING ABOUT

Aloha
PUBLISHERS
Books & Stories by Paul M. Kramer

WORRY IS NOT WORTH WORRYING ABOUT by Paul M. Kramer

Aloha Publishers LLC
848 North Rainbow Boulevard, #4738
Las Vegas, NV 89107
www.alohapublishers.com

Inquiries, comments or further information are available at, www. alohapublishers.com.

Illustrations by Vippu Kukreja
Audio by Charly Espina Takahama charly@pmghawaii.com
Collaborator, Co-Editor, Cynthia Kress Kramer

I would like to acknowledge and say thank you to Dr. Colleen Cummings, a children's anxiety expert who critiqued the original text of this book. Having the benefit of Dr. Cummings' valuable recommendations, the finalized copy of this book was vastly improved.

ISBN 13 (EAN): 978-1-941095-12-6
Library of Congress Control Number (LCCN): 2014945491
Printed in Guangzhou, China. Production date: September 2014 Cohort: Batch 1

WORRY IS NOT WORTH WORRYING ABOUT

by Paul M. Kramer

Aloha

PUBLISHERS
Books & Stories by Paul M. Kramer

This is a story about something you cannot see.
Something you cannot hear that has no smell.
It's about something that has no taste that you cannot touch.
It's something you surely cannot eat,
for if it was, it would certainly not be a treat.

What if bananas could dance?

What if elephants could read?

What if cucumbers could sing?

What if a boat couldn't float?

What if your dog eats the remote?

Would anyone think less of you if you weren't perfect
in every way?

Would you worry if you couldn't fly like a butterfly?

Would you worry if you couldn't speak Chinese?

Would you worry if you didn't wear your hair in a braid?

What if your aunt never went to a parade?

What if you weren't a genius?

What if your uncle hated cooking, would anyone care if he weren't a famous chef?

Would you worry if your mom or dad were not the president?

What if you weren't a kid and you were older?

What if hot summer days were colder?

What if John was uncoordinated and wasn't good at playing sports?

What if Jennifer wasn't quite as pretty as Denise and was worried she wouldn't be liked?

What if Jennifer and Denise traded places and now Denise wasn't as pretty as Jennifer?

Jennifer would probably tell Denise that being liked is more than how pretty you look.

She might also say that a pretty cover doesn't necessarily guarantee a good book.

Did you know that many kids worry about not getting good grades?

They worry about not measuring up to someone else's expectations.

Some kids worry about bullies and being bullied.

Kids worry about being too small.

They also worry about being too tall.

Wouldn't you tell someone who was worried about being too short that they are no less of a person?

Wouldn't you tell a friend that there's no shame if you don't get A's as long as you try your best?

If you knew that someone was being bullied, wouldn't you suggest they get help?

Wouldn't you tell someone who was very tall that there are many advantages in being tall?

Wouldn't it be nice if kids realized how unique and special they are, regardless of whether they're large or small?

What if you were worried about having too many pimples?

Kids worry about their parents breaking up.

What if someone was sick or had an accident?

What if your family had trouble paying the bills, what would they do?

What if your family had to move and leave their friends behind, has that ever happened to you?

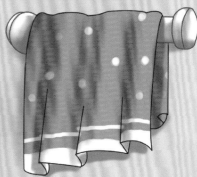

Some kids get more pimples than other kids when they get older, eating less junk food and washing their face helps, worrying does not.

It's never good for children when their parents separate or divorce, but that won't stop their kids from being happy and becoming successful.

People who get sick and have accidents usually heal and get better.

Change happens for reasons we don't always understand, but sometimes change leads to good things.

We should hope for the best and have faith that we will succeed in whatever life brings.

What if you thought about what worry really is?

Worrying is being afraid of thoughts that you imagine could happen, that you're afraid might happen, that you don't want to happen.

Have you ever worried about anything that didn't begin with what if?

Worrying more than is necessary or that is normal is a waste of your time and energy.

Too much worrying can make you feel uncomfortable and create anxiety.

It's normal to worry occasionally, but worrying too much is not good for anyone.

How can worrying about something help you if what you're worrying about doesn't happen?

How can being worried help you if what you are worrying about actually does happen?

Excessive worrying will make you uptight and cause you stress.

Worrying will not make you feel better or change negative thoughts into positive thoughts, and will not bring you happiness.

You shouldn't stop being concerned, but worrying will not make your problems disappear.

Try to figure out logical solutions to help solve what you're worried about.

Have faith and believe that you and your family can do whatever needs to be done if something unexpected happens.

If you try to be the best you can be and do the best you can do.

You'll have less to worry about and you'll be a much happier you.

So don't worry, be happy!

WORRY

Agonizing and obsessing over what ifs,
a pessimistic state of mind,
dwelling upon what may or may not happen,
fearing possibilities of every kind.

Worry is the brother and sister of anxiety.
Creating apprehension, uneasiness and stress,
worry causes us to be ill at ease,
it is an inhibitor of joy and happiness.

Worry knows no optimism.
It's not a necessity or a requirement.
We need not choose to embrace it.
Do not let it diminish the quality of our life.

"Don't worry, be happy"

Paul M. Kramer

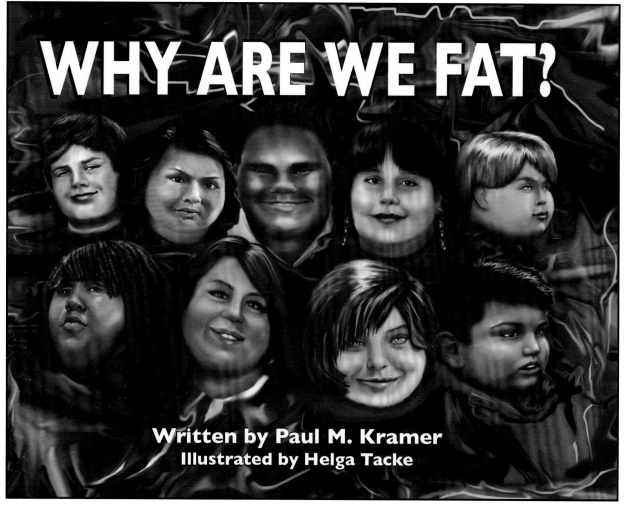

This book attempts to motivate and encourage children of all ages to develop strategies to turn bad eating habits into good ones and learn how to become dependent free from foods they have become addicted to.

Childhood obesity often leads to adult obesity which significantly increases the risk of chronic diseases such as diabetes, high blood pressure and heart disease.

"This generation of American children is the first in 200 years who have shorter life expectancies than their parents, and the major cause is obesity."

– Kathleen Sebelius, Former US Secretary of Health and Human Services.

Being overweight or obese does not make someone less of a person. They are still worthwhile and they really do matter. Unless someone has a medical condition beyond their control, other than food addiction, it is my belief that they have the ability to prevent and reverse obesity.

ISBN: 978-0-9819745-1-4, retail price: $16.95, size: 9" x 7"

Other Books Available by Paul M. Kramer

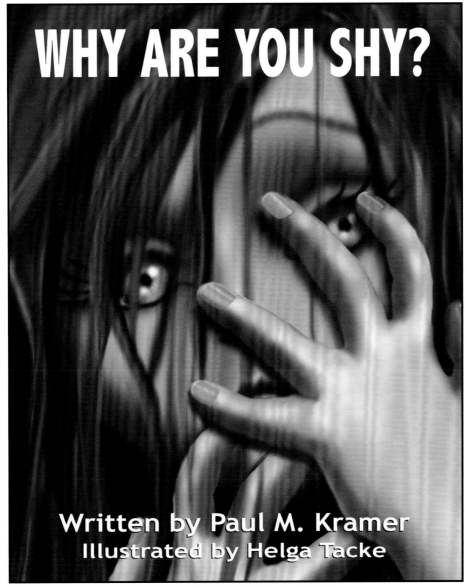

Have you or someone in your family been more than just mildly shy where it has negatively affected the quality of life? This book that is written in rhyme will entertain you and share some simple and easy steps to gain more confidence. After practicing some of the steps, it will become progressively easier to be able to talk to people and look them in the eye.

ISBN: 978-1-941095-10-2, retail price: $15.95, size: 8" x 10"

About the Author

Paul M. Kramer lives in Hawaii on the beautiful island of Maui with his wife Cindy and their son Lukas. Paul was born and raised in New York City.

Mr. Kramer's books attempt to reduce stress and anxiety and resolve important issues children face in their everyday lives. His books are often written in rhyme. They are entertaining, inspirational, educational and easy to read. One of his goals is to increase the child's sense of self worth.

He has written books on various subjects such as bullying, divorce, sleep deprivation, worrying, shyness, and weight issues.

Mr. Kramer has appeared on "Good Morning America," "The Doctors," "CNN Live" as well as several other Television Shows in the United States and Canada. He's been interviewed and aired on many radio programs including the British Broadcasting System and has had countless articles written about his work in major newspapers and magazines throughout the world.

More information about this book and Paul M. Kramer's other books are available on his website at www.alohapublishers.com.